My Rainy Day Rocket Ship

Markette Sheppard

art by

Charly Palmer

A Denene Millner Book

Simon & Schuster Books for Young Readers
New York   London   Toronto   Sydney   New Delhi

SIMON & SCHUSTER BOOKS FOR YOUNG READERS

An imprint of Simon & Schuster Children's Publishing Division

1230 Avenue of the Americas, New York, New York 10020

SIMON & SCHUSTER BOOKS FOR YOUNG READERS is a trademark of Simon & Schuster, Inc.

For information about special discounts for bulk purchases, please contact Simon & Schuster

Special Sales at 1-866-506-1949 or business@simonandschuster.com.

The Simon & Schuster Speakers Bureau can bring authors to your live event.

For more information or to book an event, contact the Simon & Schuster Speakers Bureau

at 1-866-248-3049 or visit our website at www.simonspeakers.com.

Book design by Tom Daly

The text for this book was set in Aila.

The illustrations for this book were rendered in acrylic on watercolor paper.

Manufactured in China • 0220 SCP • First Edition

2 4 6 8 10 9 7 5 3 1

Library of Congress Cataloging-in-Publication Data

Names: Sheppard, Markette, author. | Palmer, Charly, illustrator.

Title: My rainy day rocket ship / Markette Sheppard ; illustrated by Charly Palmer.

Description: First edition. | New York : Simon & Schuster Books for Young Readers, [2020] |

Audience: Ages 4-8. | Audience: Grades pre-3. | Summary: Told in rhyming text, a young

African American boy, stuck inside on a rainy day, uses his imagination to create a

rocket ship out of a rocking chair and takes off on an trip to a distant planet.

Identifiers: LCCN 2019025776 (print) | LCCN 2019025777 (ebook) |

ISBN 9781534461772 (hardcover) | ISBN 9781534461789 (ebook)

Subjects: LCSH: Space ships—Juvenile fiction. | Imagination—Juvenile fiction. |

African American boys—Juvenile fiction. | Stories in rhyme. | Picture books for children. |

CYAC: Stories in rhyme. | Space ships—Fiction. | Imagination—Fiction. |

African Americans—Fiction. | LCGFT: Stories in rhyme. | Picture books.

Classification: LCC PZ8.3.S5525 My 2020 (print) | LCC PZ8.3.S5525 (ebook) | DDC 813.6 [E]—dc23

LC record available at https://lccn.loc.gov/2019025776

LC ebook record available at https://lccn.loc.gov/2019025777

For my son, Wesley—
may you always reach for the stars . . .
and for my husband, Damon—
thank you for always lifting me up to the moon . . .
and for children with big imaginations
and boundless creativity
—M. S.

For all the image makers and dreamers out there—
live fearlessly, love openly, give freely, and practice patience;
in return, the universe will reward you with peace and joy
—C. P.

Mom says it's too rainy
to play outside today,
so I'll have to find
my fun another way.

I could get in some
laughs with inside toys—
cars and games that
bring much joy.

But I've been there and done that stuff.

Today I'll make something **really** tough.

Like a whole new world
in a different place—
a galaxy off in
outer space!

I'll need a rocket
to get me there.
Hmm . . . how about
this rocking chair?

And I'll need a super launching pad.

This will require some tools from Dad.

A cardboard box
and a bunch of socks!

These will surely
serve me well.
On this mission,
I cannot fail.

Now let me see
about a space suit.

These swimming trunks
and goggles should do.

Of course, astronauts
need a flag.
Perhaps I can use
Mom's old dishrag.

Now if I can just
get Mom to turn
off the light.

This astronaut's crew
is ready for flight.

Dad does a countdown from
behind the couch.

5, 4, 3, 2, 1

Mom makes sure
I don't feel an ouch.

Zoom, zoom, zoom

all the way from
the living room.

Down the hall,
riding on a broom.

Prepare for landing
on Planet **XYZ**.
It's a safe arrival in
my **B-E-D**…

also known as the
Land of **ZZZZZZ**s.